ECO RANGERS

RANGERS

PELICAN IN PERIL

For Gerda, who loves pelicans.

NEW FRONTIER PUBLISHING

American edition published in 2020
by New Frontier Publishing USA,
an imprint of New Frontier Publishing Europe Ltd.
www.newfrontierpublishing.us

First published in the UK in 2019
by New Frontier Publishing Europe Ltd
Uncommon, 126 New King's Rd, Fulham, London SW6 4LZ
www.newfrontierpublishing.co.uk

ISBN: 978-1-912858-84-2

Illustrated by Aśka, www.askaillustration.com
Text copyright © 2019, 2020 Candice Lemon-Scott
Illustrations copyright © 2019, 2020 New Frontier Publishing
The moral right of the author has been asserted.

Distributed in the United States and Canada by Lerner Publishing Group Inc
241 First Avenue North, Minneapolis, MN 55401 USA
www.lernerbooks.com

Library of Congress Catalogue-in-Publication Data Available

Edited by Stephanie Stahl
Designed by Rachel Lawston

Printed in China

The paper and board used in this book
are made from wood from responsible sources.

FSC
www.fsc.org
MIX
Paper from
responsible sources
FSC® C130668

1 3 5 7 9 10 8 6 4 2

ECO RANGERS
PELICAN IN PERIL

CANDICE LEMON-SCOTT

Illustrated by Aśka

EBONY

Hi everyone, I'm Ebony! I'm twelve years old. I like spending time in nature, rescuing animals, or riding my bike to go off on an adventure. I'm super independent, but sometimes I jump right in without thinking and that can get me into trouble! I love being an Eco Ranger because I get to solve mysteries!

JAY

I'm Jay, Ebony's best friend and next-door neighbor. I'm eleven years old. I like making jokes and have a bit of a sweet tooth … especially when it comes to cake! I also love nature and helping out at the wildlife hospital. Being an Eco Ranger is so much fun because I can look after animals and make sure they are safe.

"Loser buys lunch!" Ebony cried with excitement.

She jumped off her bike and raced down the sandy pathway toward the beach. Jay pulled his towel out of the milk crate that was strapped on the back of his bike. He pushed his glasses against his nose and chased after her.

Ebony was in the lead as she reached the shoreline, breathing in the salty air. She raced along the water's edge, her messy brown hair blowing around her face. She could hear Jay puffing along behind her like a steam train. She glanced back, laughing as his beach towel billowed out behind him like a parachute.

"Do we always have to race to the pier?" he complained, between breaths.

Ebony and Jay had been next-door neighbors, and best friends, for as long as she could remember. He was fun to hang out with and she could always beat him in a running race!

Without slowing, Ebony glanced behind her again. The grin on her face vanished as she tripped and landed against something hard. Ouch! She stared at her tanned knee. She had grazed it, and it started stinging straight away. She looked down to see what she'd fallen on. *It's a metal drum half-buried in the sand*, she thought. *Maybe it has washed up from the sea.*

Jay ran past her, but Ebony wasn't out of the race yet! She picked herself up and took off again.

"I won! Ha, you have to buy me lunch now," cheered Jay, who had reached the pier first.

Ebony caught up with Jay. He was bending over with his hands on his knees like he'd just run a marathon. Then she looked up and saw something in the water.

"Oh, no!" she cried. "What's that?"

Jay stood up. "You mean the cruise ship?"

The huge white liner sat anchored in the harbor. Ebony still couldn't get used to it turning up in their coast town every few weeks, since it had started touring several months ago. It brought in crowds of noisy tourists who didn't seem to notice the nature that was all around them. And there was always a line at their favorite burger place now, when they went there. The conservation center had much more work to do now tourists often trampled the fragile grasses that kept the dunes intact and left garbage on the beaches. Ever since the school summer vacation had started, Ebony and Jay had been helping out at the center with beach clean-ups and tree planting. Now they were busier than ever. Ebony didn't mean the cruise ship, though.

"No, that!" she yelled and pointed at the black sludge forming a dark, greasy layer over the sea.

"What is it?" Jay said, grimacing.

"I don't know, but we should tell the conservation center," Ebony replied.

"You're right," Jay agreed. "We have to get there straight away. Then we could have an early lunch," he said, with a grin.

"Do you ever think of anything other than your belly?" Ebony smiled.

"Not really." He shrugged and rubbed his stomach through his oversized T-shirt.

"We need to see what it looks like from the pier first and how far out that black water goes." Ebony made her way to the pier. She hoped they would know what that black stuff was at the center. The sea had never looked like this before.

When she got halfway down the wooden platform, she stopped at the steel steps to the pontoon.

"I want to get closer," she said to Jay.

Her friend nodded and she made her way carefully down the slippery, wet stairs. Water lapped through the slits. She could see the dark smear more clearly now. It sat on top of the water.

As Ebony reached the bottom of the pontoon she noticed there was something lying in the corner. It was a black bundle. She stepped closer, and the shape moved.

She screamed and leaped back in fright. Jay came running down the steps, his sneakers clanking on the metal surface. Ebony stood with her hand clasped to her mouth. In front of her was a black feathered mound, like a big, fluffy pillow.

"What is that?" Jay cried.

"I don't know. I thought it was a pile of garbage, but then it moved," Ebony said.

The two friends edged closer to it. Ebony could now see long feathers. Big, solid wings were pressed against the creature's body. It was covered in sticky, black goop the same color as the sludge she'd seen in the sea.

"It looks like a bird," Ebony said.

She walked up to it, slowly and carefully. She could see part of a long, peachy-colored bill and one very large, black eye staring straight at her.

"It's a pelican," Ebony gasped.

"Is it okay?" Jay asked.

"I don't know. It hasn't moved much."

She stepped in closer until she could almost reach out and touch the gigantic bird. Ebony had always thought pelicans were such interesting creatures. They looked a bit prehistoric, like something that belonged back in the time of the dinosaurs. She could see its big, gray feet curled up under its feathers. It made her think of all the times she had seen pelicans gliding down to the water, their wings stretched wide. Their webbed feet would skim across the water, acting like brakes. This one was covered in thick, greasy, black sludge, though. The bird smelled of fuel, like when her mom was filling up the car at the service station.

Ebony reached out to touch the pelican but it raised its great wings, knocking her sideways. Unhurt, Ebony stood back up and shook herself off.

"What are we going to do with it?" Jay asked, edging closer to the gigantic bird to see if it was injured.

It didn't move but, just as he got close enough to touch it, the pelican opened its wings and Jay stepped to the side, slipping on the edge of the jetty.

"Careful!" Ebony cried. She reached out

to grab him but as she grasped Jay's towel, it slipped from his shoulders.

"Help!" Jay yelled, falling into the water below.

Ebony was left holding just his towel. She ran to the edge to see Jay paddling his arms in the water. He pushed himself forward in his heavy clothes, grabbed his glasses that were slowly sinking beside him, then swam to the edge of the pontoon. He pulled himself up on the ladder.

Ebony grabbed hold of his arm and helped pull her soggy friend up. He put his glasses back on, panting. She wrapped the towel around his shoulders.

"Are you okay?" Ebony asked.

"I guess," Jay gasped, blinking through his wet glasses.

Seeing him completely soaked with his hair plastered to his head, Ebony started laughing.

"That pelican's a menace," Jay said,

making Ebony laugh even more.

The pelican made a kind of crowing sound, like a rooster with a cold.

"Did you hear that?" Ebony said.

She moved closer again. The bird tried to stand but seemed too weak to push its large body up. It slumped back down.

"I wish we had some food to give it. Anyone who gives *me* something to eat is my next best friend," Jay commented.

"We don't have anything with us, though. Unless you have a fish hiding in your pocket!" Ebony smiled.

"Only these. No good for birds," Jay replied, pulling out some lint-covered chocolates. He picked a few of them up and popped them into his mouth.

"Ewww," Ebony cried.

Jay shrugged and held out his hand, "Want one?"

Ebony shook her head and crouched down near the pelican. She looked into its huge black eyes and the bird stared back at her. It was as though it was asking her for help but she had no idea what to do. Standing, it would be nearly as tall as her. How were they going to rescue a bird of that size?

"Stay still," Jay whispered.

Ebony didn't move. The pelican stretched out its bill and rested it right on the sore spot where she'd grazed her knee. Ouch! Not a feather on its body moved but it looked around as though taking everything in.

Crouching in an uncomfortable position, Ebony was forced to move, startling the pelican so it lifted its bill off her leg again. It blinked its eyes and made a low sound so quiet she could barely hear it.

"We have to get it to the wildlife hospital," she said.

"And fast!" Jay agreed.

"Jay, you're the biggest and strongest. You should be the one to carry the pelican." Ebony smiled.

"Why do I get all the tough jobs?"

Ebony pulled out her mom's old cell phone. She had taken it with her ever since she and Jay had been allowed to go to the beach on their own. Ebony had added a hot-pink cover and now it looked more like hers. She was only supposed to use it if there was an emergency. She thought this would count as one for sure. She texted her mom.

Hi Mom, Be home soon. Jay and I found pelican by the pier. Taking to conservation center. Ebony xx

Jay handed his towel to Ebony, bent down to the pelican and stretched his arms out to pick it up, as if he was the scoop on an earthmover. But as soon as he touched the pelican, it lifted its huge wings and whacked him in the shoulder. Jay turned to the side but then the pelican hit him in the cheek, knocking his glasses off his face. He stumbled over his feet, stepped back—and fell in the water again.

"Jay!" Ebony cried.

"There's no way that bird's going to let me pick it up. And now I'm covered in this awful black goo, too," Jay said, as he pulled himself back onto the pontoon for the second time.

Ebony couldn't argue. He looked almost as messy as the bird now.

"You look like a zombie." She laughed. "And you smell like one, too."

"Thanks a lot," Jay grumbled.

"What are we going to do about the pelican?" Ebony asked.

"We'll just have to go to the center first and get someone to come out to get it."

"It could be too late by then," she argued, looking at the sick bird.

Jay rubbed the towel over his sticky arms and legs, getting off as much of the goo as he could. He looked human again once he was dried off. That gave Ebony an idea.

"Let me try something first."

Ebony took the towel from Jay, who groaned that he was now cold, and carefully wrapped it around the bird. She put her arms over its body, holding its wings down gently, and lifted it. She was surprised the pelican was so light when it was such a big bird.

"Wow, the pelican likes that!" Jay said.

Ebony smiled proudly. "I'm going to name it Poseidon."

"Poseidon?"

"Yeah, you know, after the Greek god of the sea," she said. "Come on, let's get Poseidon to the conservation center."

The friends walked slowly back up the sandy path to their bikes, Ebony carrying Poseidon all the way. The pelican wriggled in her arms, tickling her with its feathers as it tried to get down. Ebony hushed the bird until it calmed.

She passed the spot where she had tripped. That was weird. There were tire tracks leading away from the half-buried drum. It looked like someone had deliberately dumped the garbage on the beach. People didn't think about what harm they were doing to the environment sometimes. She looked down at Poseidon. *Like to this poor pelican*, she thought.

Ebony stopped when she reached her bike, realizing how far they were from home. How were they going to get the pelican back? It was too far to walk and a bird couldn't ride a bike!

"Why don't I go and get help while you stay here with Poseidon?" Jay suggested.

"That will take too long," Ebony said.

"Maybe we can put it in my milk crate, then?" he said.

Ebony looked at the crate tied to his bike. "Good idea!" she agreed.

She placed the bird down gently in the crate. Poseidon looked like a bird too big for its nest. The friends laughed.

"Sorry it's not very comfortable, Poseidon, but we've got to get you some help," Ebony said.

Jay straddled his bike but as soon as he did Poseidon tried to get out of the crate. Jay quickly jumped off again.

"This will never work," he groaned.

"Let me try it," Ebony suggested.

Jay moved aside as they swapped bikes. Ebony gently stroked the pelican's back. The bird folded its wings in, settling into the crate.

"It's going to look pretty funny pedaling with a pelican!" Ebony said, touching Poseidon's head gently.

"At least you're not going to be picked on for the rest of your life. If anyone sees me riding a pink girls' bike home, I'll never be able to show my face at school again," Jay sighed.

Ebony and Jay pedaled to the conservation center and made their way to the wildlife hospital building. Ebony waved at the gardener who was watering plants as they cycled past. His eyes widened when he noticed there was a pelican on the bike. Then he realized, too late, he was accidentally hosing his boot.

"Now I've seen everything," he laughed.

When they got to the wildlife hospital, Jay ran to the front desk and explained everything, while his friends waited outside. Shortly after, two white-coated vets came out of the double glass doors at the front.

"Goodness! It's a pelican," one of the vets commented. It was Doctor Battacharjee, but everyone called her Doctor Bat for short. She'd been working at the hospital ever since she had become a vet and she was the kindest person Ebony knew. Her black hair, with streaks of gray, was pulled back in a ponytail. She might be small in height but she was huge of heart. If anyone could fix Poseidon, it would be Doctor Bat.

"We found it at the pier," Ebony explained.

"You've done a fantastic job bringing it here. We'll do our very best to look after this poor bird," said Doctor Bat.

Ebony smiled. Doctor Tan spoke next. The younger, taller vet crouched down to be closer to Ebony's height.

"Who's this?" Doctor Tan asked, looking at the pelican kindly.

"This is Poseidon," Ebony said.

"What a great name for a water bird," he said.

"What's this black stuff all over it?" Jay asked. "It was in the water as well."

Doctor Bat lifted the towel covering Poseidon, lightly touching the black goo. Her frown lines deepened when she looked at the pelican more closely.

"This is not good," she said, shaking her head. "It's oil."

"That's why the pelican's in such a state. He'll be cold without clean feathers to keep him warm. He's dehydrated, too," Doctor Tan said.

"He?" Ebony asked.

"Yes, this is a male."

"How can you tell?"

"They're much larger than the females."

"It's lucky you found him when you did," Doctor Bat said. "Let's take the pelican in and get him cleaned up."

Ebony and Jay nodded.

"Will he be all right?" Ebony asked.

"He should be fine. With a bit of help from us."

"Where could the oil have come from?" Jay asked.

The vets looked at each other, concerned.

"Oil spills come from leaks on ships. They're a disaster for the environment and wildlife. It can take years to clean it all up completely," Doctor Bat said.

"Could the oil leak have come from the cruise ship?" Ebony wondered.

"Yes, possibly," Doctor Bat said. "We'll find out more later. Right now, we need to help this bird."

Doctor Bat reached to take Poseidon from the crate but he started flapping his wings and made a strange gurgling sound at the back of his throat. Ebony tried to hold the bike steady. The vet stepped back. Poseidon pulled his wings back in and slumped into the crate again. When Ebony touched the top of his head gently, the bird stared at her and he calmed down.

"We don't want to cause him farther injury," Doctor Bat said. "Doctor Tan, do you want to give it a try?"

The vet nodded and Doctor Bat moved aside. Doctor Tan reached forward very slowly, edging closer with one outstretched hand. Poseidon kept perfectly still, as if he was a sculpture, but when the vet got that bit closer he started whipping his bill from side to side. Doctor Tan moved back and Poseidon let his bill fold in again, against himself.

"We don't want to put him under any more stress," Doctor Bat said.

"What do you want to do? Sedate him?" Doctor Tan asked.

"It could put him at risk, as he's already very weak," replied Doctor Bat. "We may have to take the chance though. He won't last the night with that oil on him."

"Why don't you get Ebony to carry him in?" Jay suggested.

Doctor Bat started to protest.

"She's the only one who can get close to him," he added.

"Hmm, do you think you could?" Doctor Bat asked Ebony, looking at her with a slightly worried expression.

"Yes," Ebony said, straight away. "He's not heavy, just a bit awkward to carry."

"Okay." Doctor Bat nodded. "But if that doesn't work, we'll have to sedate him."

Ebony nodded, and Poseidon stayed calm as she lifted him out.

"Okay, good. Now, hold him with one arm across his wings and in front of his body," Doctor Bat explained.

Ebony folded her right arm over him.

"Good! Now use your other hand to gently push his bill down. Make sure you don't cover his nostrils, or he won't be able to breathe. He'll feel much more comfortable and be easier to hold then."

Ebony did as she was told. The vet was right, it was much easier to hold him this way and he barely moved as she took a few steps toward the vets. She followed them into the wildlife hospital.

"He is certainly happy to have you taking care of him," Doctor Tan said.

"It's incredible," Doctor Bat agreed. "You are both amazing at looking after the environment. We have two real Eco Rangers here."

Ebony smiled at Jay. She liked the sound of that.

They followed the vets through the front lobby. It was bustling with wildlife officers rushing around, helping sick and injured animals. The phone was ringing non-stop. Even though it was so busy, everyone working with the animals had a smile on their faces.

Judy at the front desk kindly said hello to Ebony who was carrying the pelican.

"This one's a bit urgent, Judy," Doctor Bat said, her smile fading for a moment. "We'll take care of the paperwork later."

"I see." Judy nodded, wrapping her finger nervously around one of her strawberry-blonde curls.

"Can you ring the conservation center in Building A, though, please?" Doctor Bat continued. "There's been an oil spill. We need to find out what happened and alert authorities."

"Oh, dear," Judy replied, turning pale, her spatter of freckles standing out. "I'll get straight onto them."

Ebony wondered how the spill could have happened. How did a big cruise ship leak oil? Poseidon trembled under her arms. There was no time to think about it now. They had to get the pelican cleaned up first.

The vets made their way down the hallway, passing by the glass windows of the treatment rooms. Ebony caught a glimpse of steel tables, trays full of equipment, and stands with bags filled with liquids. In one, she saw a kangaroo being operated on.

Doctor Bat led them to one of the end rooms and pushed open the door. Ebony placed Poseidon gently on the table, still wrapped in the towel.

"First, we need to rehydrate him," Doctor Bat explained.

The vets got a bag of the hydrating

solution and attached a feeding tube to it. They opened Poseidon's bill gently and put the tube down his throat. Ebony and Jay watched as Poseidon guzzled down the liquid. When it was done, Doctor Bat explained it was time to clean him up.

"This is where we'll need you to help."

"Of course. I'll just text Mom to let her know," Ebony said.

"My parents aren't home till later, so I can stay too," Jay said. "There is one problem, though."

Doctor Bat raised her eyebrows.

"We haven't had any lunch."

"Hey! You're just trying to make sure I buy you lunch because you won the race," Ebony complained.

"Well, we have a pelican to save now. We have to keep our strength up," Jay joked.

Doctor Bat burst into laughter. "No problem. Why don't you kids go and get us all burgers and fries from the harbor.

It's on us for helping out."

Ebony gave Jay a cheeky grin.

Jay and Ebony cycled down to the burger place at the harbor. Standing at the counter, Jay read out the order for the vets that he had scrawled on a piece of paper. The teenager behind the counter told them it would be ready in fifteen minutes.

They waited outside while their burgers were being cooked. Ebony grimaced at the cruise box office, which was next door. She thought back to what Doctor Bat had said about the spill possibly coming from the cruise ship. While they were waiting, a man walked out of the office. He had slicked-back dark hair and was dressed in a business suit. He was talking on his cell phone. Ebony couldn't hear much of what he was saying but she was sure she heard the words "oil" and "clean up."

Ebony nudged Jay and they moved closer to listen in.

"No, it's okay, the news is reporting it was an accidental leak..." The man was whispering urgently into his phone.

Jay and Ebony looked at each other, frowning.

"Yes, yes, keep dumping the waste ... no, don't empty the drums straight from the ship, stupid ... careful with the oil. Yes, keep filling the drums... What? I am the cruise ship manager, and you'll do as I say!"

The man jabbed the "off" button on his phone and rammed it into his pocket. He looked up. Ebony saw him catch sight of her staring. She spun Jay around and they fast-walked back into the burger place.

"Did you hear that?" Jay said.

"Shhh," Ebony said, half whispering. "Yes. The oil did come from the cruise ship. Worse, from what he said I think they are deliberately dumping that oil. There was no leak."

She thought of the drum she had tripped over at the beach. Had the cruise ship dumped oil out of that drum? But if it had, it didn't explain the tire marks.

"Number forty-three! Order's ready!" The teenager behind the counter yelled out.

When Ebony and Jay got back to the wildlife hospital, they told the vets what they'd overheard outside the cruise box office. Ebony was talking at full speed and Jay with a mouthful of fries.

"I know what you think you heard," Doctor Bat said softly, "but it sounds to me that the cruise ship manager was just talking about waste removal. Maybe he was just angry at his staff for not doing a good job."

"Did he actually say they were dumping the oil?" Doctor Tan asked.

"He used all those words," Ebony argued.

"But not together, in one sentence?"

"No, but it sounded bad," Jay said, shoving more fries into his mouth.

"I'm sure a big cruise liner wouldn't deliberately dump oil into the sea." Doctor Bat looked at Ebony and Jay.

"It just wouldn't make sense for them to do that," Doctor Tan added.

"I fell over a half-buried drum at the beach," Ebony said. "It could have been an oil drum."

"All cruise ships fill their drums with waste oil."

"What is waste oil?" Jay asked.

"It's the leftover oil from running the engine. The ships have to pay a fee to take it to a local waste removal center when they're ashore. I'm sure that drum you found was just one of those that had already been emptied at the waste center."

"But why was it on the beach?"

"I don't know." Doctor Bat paused. "But the reports coming in to the conservation center are that the oil in the sea was from a leak, and they're fixing it now. I'm sure that's all it was and we should just concentrate on cleaning up the oil as quickly as we can. Before more wildlife like Poseidon are caught up in it. Speaking of which," she added, "I think those tubs will be ready for your friend now. Come and we'll show you how to clean him up."

Ebony followed the vets, but still she was sure the cruise liner was up to something. And she was determined to find out what!

Ebony and Jay spent all afternoon cleaning Poseidon. It was a big job. The vets had filled a tub with a mixture of water and special, gentle soap for animals. They gave the kids some gloves and showed them how to scrub Poseidon's feathers using a toothbrush. Doctor Tan also handed them some cotton swabs and taught them how to use it for the soft spots around his head and eyes. The vet explained that whenever the water got too dirty, they should move Poseidon to a tub with clean water and soap, and start cleaning him again until the water stayed clear.

Once they knew what to do, the vets left them to work. Ebony held Poseidon while Jay got the next tub ready. After twelve tubs, and aching arms and backs, Poseidon was all clean. But the job wasn't quite done yet. Next, they had to hose him off and dry him. Poseidon looked funny as he sat under the special wildlife hairdryer.

"You've done a fantastic job, kids," Doctor Bat said, when they showed off their sparkling clean friend.

"Where will we let him go? We can't take him back to where he was," Ebony said, thinking of the oil-covered sea.

"It's not as easy as that, I'm afraid," Doctor Tan explained. "He won't be ready for flight yet. We need to hold him here and keep him well fed until he's strong enough to go back into the wild."

"Yes." Doctor Bat nodded. "The only problem is that now we all have lots of work to do cleaning up after this horrible oil spill, so we're going to need extra help to look after your special friend. Do you think you could come back tomorrow afternoon to feed him for us … Eco Rangers?" the vet said, with a smile.

Ebony and Jay both nodded. "We'd love to!"

"We'll keep him in the hospital room for tonight and move him out to the enclosures when you come around in the afternoon." Doctor Bat smiled. "Make sure you get some good rest tonight. Tomorrow is going to be a busy day indeed!"

Little did Ebony know they'd be back at the hospital sooner than they'd expected.

Ebony and Jay dropped their bikes at the front entrance and raced through the doors of the wildlife hospital the next afternoon. Judy, the receptionist, gave them a worried glance and quickly waved them through to the treatment rooms.

Ebony swallowed nervously. Then she heard a bang, a crash, another loud bang, and a strange twang. When they reached Poseidon's room, she peered through the glass window. She saw him stumbling around on a set of scales as a veterinary nurse tried to calm him down. He turned and one wing hit a container of cotton balls. They fell from the bench and scattered like large snowflakes all over the floor. He turned the other way and got his leg caught in a power cable. It twisted around him and he became more and more tangled. Finally, there was a huge crash as a light fell to the ground.

"Wow! It's messier than my bedroom," Jay cried.

"He's really going to hurt himself," Ebony said.

Doctor Bat appeared, with Doctor Tan trailing behind.

"Ebony? Do you think you might be able to try and calm him down?" Doctor Tan asked.

"I'll see if I can," she replied.

"Come straight back out if he won't settle, though. He's very upset right now. I don't want you to get hurt," Doctor Bat said.

"I'll be careful," Ebony said.

Ebony slowly opened the door to the room. She peered in. Poseidon now had a vet's mask sitting on his head and was spinning in circles. A basket of exam gloves fell to the ground and Poseidon slipped on the glove-covered floor, knocking against another tray as he did.

"Poseidon," Ebony whispered.

The bird stopped and tilted his head to one side, listening. Ebony took a small step forward as the vet nurse slipped gratefully out of the room.

"It's okay. We're helping you get better," she whispered to him.

She came a little closer until she could reach out and touch him. She stroked his long, feathered neck. Ebony could understand how Poseidon must be feeling. Everything was so strange and different in here. There was no water or trees or sand. Just walls and windows and the smell of disinfectant.

Ebony crouched down and lifted the bird's bill onto her lap. He turned his great head to one side again and she stroked him gently.

"It's okay," Ebony said. "Soon you'll be good as new and you can go home again."

Poseidon rubbed the side of his bill against the knee she'd grazed the day before. It still hurt a bit but she didn't dare move.

The door opened slowly and Doctor Bat came in. Poseidon continued resting his bill on Ebony's knee.

"Ow! Why does he always end up on my sore spot?"

"Ahh, now I see," Doctor Bat said, softly.

"See what?" Ebony asked.

"I think that might be the reason he'll only calm down for you."

"What's that?" Jay said, coming up behind the vet.

"He has something in common with you, Ebony. He was hurt and so were you.

That's why he trusts you... Do you think you could take him home to be his wildlife carers until he's well enough to be returned to the wild?"

"Of course!" Ebony and Jay agreed.

A few days later, Poseidon's part-time home was ready. Ebony, Jay, and their families, as well as the vets, had all helped create the pelican's enclosure in Ebony's backyard, since hers had the most space. Jay's parents had brought over their old chicken coop to use. Doctor Tan gave them a heat lamp so Poseidon wouldn't get too cold. They put some old towels down on the ground to make it comfortable. They even found a big log from a tree that had fallen by the side of their yard, and brought it over. That way, when Poseidon was strong enough, he'd have a perch to sit on. Lastly, to make him feel more at home, Jay added a few smaller branches. Ebony went over to the tap, attached the hose and filled up the old inflatable pool she'd had when she was little.

"We've really done a great job setting up a pelican home in Ebony's backyard," Jay's dad said, smiling.

"Now all we need is our feathered guest to enjoy his new home," Jay's mom said.

Ebony picked up Poseidon from the back of the hospital truck and carried him toward his enclosure. She knew if he settled in well he would get better faster. Jay swung the enclosure door open and Ebony stepped inside, carrying the pelican. She crouched down and gently let go of Poseidon.

"Welcome to your new home," she said.

Poseidon stood still for a moment, his big black eyes shining as though he was deciding if he liked her backyard or not. He then slowly moved his weight from foot to foot, feeling the grass beneath him.

His wings lifted and for a moment Ebony thought he didn't like it. She was worried he'd start flapping about and hurt himself again. Instead, he let his wings fall back against his body and made a calling sound, like a cross between a rooster and a duck. She laughed as he continued calling and strutting around proudly.

"Do you think he's happy with it?" Jay asked, peering inside.

"I think so," Ebony said.

"He's probably very hungry, though?" Jay suggested.

"Trust you to think that." Ebony laughed. "Doctor Bat? Doctor Tan?"

Seeing that the pelican had settled in, Ebony's mom and Jay's parents left them to take care of Poseidon. The vets carried a bucket of fish over and showed them how to hand-feed him. But when Doctor Tan held a small fish toward Poseidon, the bird backed away from him.

"He ate yesterday but now he's rejecting his food," Doctor Tan said.

"Let us try," Ebony suggested, nodding to Jay.

Ebony went up to Poseidon, patting him softly on his back. Jay took a fish, holding it by the tail above the pelican's head. This time Poseidon lifted his head and opened his bill wide. Jay dropped it in. The pelican gulped it down quickly and opened his mouth for more.

"Great work, Eco Rangers! Poseidon seems to trust both of you. Can you keep feeding him for us?" Doctor Bat asked. "We have to get back to the hospital to deal with some other animals coming in with oil on them."

"Sure," Ebony said.

"How much do we give him?" Jay asked.

"He'll stop eating when he's full enough," Doctor Bat said, and the vets left.

Ebony and Jay kept feeding Poseidon

until he paused and tilted his head. Then he started turning in circles, making the rooster-duck crowing sound in his throat again.

"I think he's okay now," Ebony giggled.

"Great! Dinner time, then?" Jay asked.

"We just fed him," Ebony said.

"I meant, is it dinner time for us? We are all eating at yours tonight."

Ebony grinned at her friend. They locked Poseidon's cage behind them, then went inside to wash their hands.

The next morning, after having spent some time with Poseidon in Ebony's backyard, the two friends rode to the wildlife hospital and back. They were a funny sight riding with Jay's bike crate filled with fish, and people pointed at them from their car windows. One passenger even took a photo of them with her phone.

Poseidon was getting stronger and eating more fish so they had to go and get some more to fill his belly. As she pedaled up the road, Ebony couldn't help thinking about the cruise ship. She still wondered what the cruise ship manager had meant when he'd said into his phone that the drums needed to be filled with oil.

When Jay screeched to a stop, she nearly banged into him.

"What are you doing?" she cried.

Jay pointed to the back of his bike. Ebony looked down. He had a flat tire.

"Oh, no!" she said.

"Want to tow me home?" he joked.

"I've got a better idea," Ebony said.

Jay and Ebony walked their bikes around the corner to the service station. Jay took his over to the air hose and started pumping up his tire. There were only a couple of cars filling up with gas. There was a big truck at the diesel pump as well. The man filling it up looked familiar. She moved a few steps closer. The man seemed out of place in his business suit, pumping diesel. As he smoothed down his already slicked-back hair, Ebony nudged Jay.

"Look who it is," she gasped.

"That's the cruise ship manager," Jay said.

The man finished filling the truck and returned the nozzle to the pump. He moved inside to pay. Ebony looked at the back of the truck. It was fully loaded, and whatever was in it was covered in a big, blue sheet of tarpaulin.

"I wonder what he's got in the back?" Ebony said.

"It all looks fishy to me," Jay joked. "Get it?"

Ebony groaned and snuck over to investigate. She looked through the glass doors of the service station and saw the man was up at the register. Crouching behind the back of the truck, she reached up and lifted the edge of the tarp. Inside there were metal drums, at least eight of them. Each drum had the word "Waste" on it, in big black lettering. Again, she thought back to the manager talking on the phone, asking someone to fill the drums with oil. Scrambling up onto the back of the truck, she was just able to lift the lid of one of the drums. It was heavy and she could only lift it a tiny bit. It was enough to see inside, though. The drum was filled with thick, oozy, black liquid. It smelled like Poseidon had the day they rescued him, only worse. It was oil!

The vets were right. The ship manager and the two men were taking their waste oil to the disposal center like they were supposed to. The oil in the sea must have been from a leak after all. She was wrong about the ship manager being up to something. Quickly, she dropped the lid back into place and jumped off the truck.

"Hey, what are you doing?"

Ebony spun around. Two men in overalls were racing toward her. They were carrying slices of pizza, but didn't notice the hot sauce dripping down their hands.

"N-n-nothing," Ebony stammered, her face now burning hot at being caught. "I, ah … sorry."

She raced back to Jay. She turned to see the cruise ship manager come running out of the service station. The two men in overalls were talking to him and pointing at Ebony.

"Quick, let's get out of here!" Ebony yelled.

They jumped on their bikes and took off. Halfway up the road, the truck went past them, spraying Ebony and Jay with gravel. *That's weird, the waste disposal center is in the opposite direction*, Ebony thought.

"Come on, Eco Ranger, let's follow them," she said.

"No way, if we're caught—" Jay began.

But Ebony was already pedaling after them, wondering what these suspicious men were up to.

Ebony rode as hard as she could after the truck but it was too fast and soon she was falling farther and farther behind it. Finally, the vehicle turned the corner toward the beach and disappeared. Ebony stopped her bike and got off. She wished she'd been able to find out where it was going. She turned around. *Where was Jay?* She couldn't see him. Maybe he'd decided not to follow her and had gone home. She got back on her bike and swung around. Then she saw Jay come around the last bend. He was pulling his bike along, his tire flat again.

"Where's the truck?" he said.

"I couldn't keep up. It turned off that road up there." Ebony sighed. "That truck is filled with waste oil drums but they didn't take it to the waste disposal center."

"No, they were heading toward the

beach," Jay agreed.

"They may be dumping the oil on the beach," Ebony said, looking worried.

She was finally sure that the ship manager was up to something!

Back at Ebony's house, the two friends fed Poseidon the fish they'd brought back from the wildlife hospital. After he was full, they made themselves some sandwiches. They took their plates into the living room and switched on the TV for a rest after their busy day. The news was on. It was boring and Ebony was about to change channels when a picture of the cruise ship came up on the screen. She turned up the volume. A reporter started speaking from in front of the cruise ship: "The cruise line manager announced today that the oil leak is now fully repaired."

The manager came on screen. He started

speaking into a microphone the reporter was holding in front of him. "We care very much for the environment and we can promise we have made every effort to ensure an oil leak never happens again. All remaining oil waste is contained in drums and has been disposed of carefully at the town's waste disposal facility."

"But he still had those waste drums in the truck with him, full of oil," Jay said.

"That manager hasn't disposed of it at all," Ebony agreed.

"He's lying to the reporter," Jay said.

The reporter thanked the manager and turned to the camera. "The ship is set to depart at two this afternoon."

"That's only an hour away," Jay said.

Ebony switched off the TV. Then she heard a scream.

The friends raced outside. Ebony found her
mom bent over, her hands over her head.

"That bird is too clever. He got out of
his enclosure," she said.

Ebony looked over at the enclosure.
The door was wide open. She must have
forgotten to lock it after they'd fed him
that morning.

"Oh, no!" Ebony said, worried.

Ebony looked at her mom, whose dark
brown hair was pulled out of her ponytail
in tufts. Poseidon had jumped on her head!

"Are you okay, Mom?" Ebony asked.

"Yes, it's the pelican I'm worried about." She was pointing at the house.

Ebony ran down the narrow gap between the side of the house and the fence with Jay, and her mom following closely behind. Some of the pot plants were overturned and the laundry basket was squashed. She noticed a shiny white patch on her pink sweater, hanging from the clothesline.

"Eww, what's that?" she said.

"Um, looks like bird poo to me," Jay replied, holding back a laugh.

Ebony gazed upwards. Poseidon was sitting on top of the clothesline. He started making a clacking sound.

"How are we going to get him down from there?" her mom said.

"I'll see if I can get him to come to me."

Ebony's mom nodded.

Ebony reached up to the top of the clothesline and stretched out her arm toward Poseidon, but he was too far away.

"Can you give me a boost, Jay?" she asked.

Jay bent down and Ebony stepped onto his back.

"It's okay," she said softly, stretching her arm out a little farther until she could touch the pelican. She stroked his feathers. "Come on down. Please," she said.

Poseidon edged forward, the clothesline wobbling as he did.

"Oh," Ebony's mom shrieked. "He's going to break it!"

Ebony whispered to Poseidon that there was no need to be scared. She kept her arms outstretched as though about to catch him. Poseidon shuffled forward until finally he stretched out his wings and half flew, half leaped to the ground. Ebony hurriedly went to grab him but he moved out of reach. Then he stopped a little farther down the side of the house. She came a bit closer but just as she got near enough to reach him he moved farther away again.

"What's he doing?" Jay asked.

"I think he wants us to follow him," Ebony said. "Keep an eye on him."

She ran inside, took her cell phone off the counter and came back out.

"Mom, I've got my phone. If he goes too far and we can't catch him, I'll text you."

"Okay, but don't go farther than the beach."

Ebony nodded then followed Jay, who was following Poseidon.

They chased Poseidon up the road. It looked like he was trying to go home, but why would he want the two friends to follow him? He made his way toward the beach and then up a sand dune. They climbed up after him and saw him standing on the other side, about halfway down. There was another pelican there. It was sitting on a nest made of twigs, grass, and feathers. Poseidon started hopping toward it and joined the other, smaller pelican. It was sitting on something.

Ebony walked up slowly. The pelican was sitting on a nest. She peeked inside. There was an egg lying in it.

"Wow! You're going to be a dad, Poseidon," Ebony said. "So that's why you were in a hurry to go home!"

Poseidon snapped at her sweater with his bill.

"What is it?" Ebony said, as she looked at the pelican. He strutted around the nest.

A thought struck her. "It's his turn for egg-sitting duties."

"What do you mean?" Jay asked.

"At school last year we learned how mom and dad pelicans take turns keeping their eggs warm in the nest," she explained. "I'd better let Mom know we're all okay." She sent her mom a text.

At beach with Poseidon. Be back soon. Ebony xx

The pelican started clucking and waddling back and forth.

"Come on," Ebony said. "Let's go home."

"What about Poseidon?" Jay said.

"I don't think he's going very far any time soon since it's his turn for egg-sitting duties."

"What do you mean?" Jay asked.

"Look!"

Poseidon was now the one sitting on the nest.

"Okay, we'll check on you again later, Poseidon," Jay laughed.

"Let's go back this way, it's faster getting back home," Ebony said, pointing to the next dune.

They went back over the dunes. It was hard work climbing through the soft sand. Sweating, Ebony took off her sweater, tying it around her waist.

Scrambling over one particularly high dune, they came to a big pool of murky water. *It's strange there is so much water here,* Ebony thought. *It hasn't rained in weeks.* She went closer and then she could see it wasn't water at all. It was oil. A big murky pool of oily waste. And it had been dumped at the dunes.

"There's something over there," Jay said. He looked through the grass. "It's a drum. It has the word "Waste" on the side."

"It's the same as the one that was in the back of that truck," Ebony said.

She'd been right, the cruise ship manager had been dumping the oil waste. But why would he do that? She came up next to Jay and rolled the drum over. It was empty.

She pulled out her cell phone and took a photo of the drum and the oily waste. Then she heard a noise. It was coming from over the dune.

"Quick! Someone's coming," she said.

Ebony and Jay crouched behind the grassy knoll. It was the two men they'd seen with the manager at the service station. They were carrying another drum. Ebony held her breath. She watched one of the men grumbling as he emptied the drum of oily waste out into the dunes. She went to yell out for him to stop, but Jay gestured for her to remain silent.

"Come on! We have to get back. We sail out in half an hour," the man said.

"But there's still another drum of waste oil to get rid of back on the ship," the second man said.

"We'll have to empty that one straight into the sea."

"The boss won't be happy if we do that."

"No one will even know it was us. The oil will all spread out in the water if we wait to empty it when the ship sails out."

Ebony couldn't believe it! How many more animals would be harmed when they dumped more oil into the sea? They had to stop the cruise ship before it left the harbor!

7

Ebony and Jay ran toward the jetty where
the cruise ship was moored. Ebony couldn't
believe how big the ship looked up close.
Even the life rafts on the side of it looked
tiny compared to the size of the ship. Rows
and rows of cabin windows gleamed like a
million eyes staring at her. Passengers were
already starting to board for departure and
looked in a hurry.

"How are we going to get on there?"
Jay asked.

He pointed to the long line of passengers.
They filed in like ants with cruise tags

around their necks, towels wrapped around shoulders, and packs on their backs.

"I don't know, but we have to get on board."

Ebony and Jay hung around the side of the pier. People were talking about their buffet breakfast, about swimming in the deck pools and how they still felt like they were rocking even though they'd been stuck in port all this time. Ebony frowned when she heard a couple whinging about staying there.

"It wasn't like this in the brochure," the man complained.

"I know," the woman agreed. "It's bad enough we've been stuck here for days, but the cruise promised white sandy beaches and water so clear you can see straight to the bottom of the sea."

"I'm demanding a refund when we get back on board," the man grumbled.

Ebony and Jay crouched by the edge of

the ship and waited for a chance to get on unnoticed, but it was too busy. Ebony's plan to get on board was never going to work. Even if she could cut the line, there was a security guard at the gangway. Just as she thought they should give up and go home, Jay nudged her.

"Now's our chance," he whispered.

He was pointing at the open gangway. The security guard was off to the side, trying to calm down a passenger who had lost her ID tag, and who was crying and yelling that she didn't want to be left behind.

"Quick!" Ebony said.

They were about to run on when Ebony realized she'd lost her sweater. It must have come untied as they ran down the pier. It was too late to look for it now. This was their one chance to get on the ship. They ran up the gangplank while the guard still had his attention on the woman, and snuck on board the ship.

"Well done!" Ebony whispered to Jay. "It's fun being Eco Rangers!"

Ebony had never seen a place so big and shiny. In every direction she looked there were stairways and passageways. She had no idea where to go, now they were there. She read her phone. They only had twenty minutes before the ship would leave port. She glanced at the walls. There was a map of the ship on one side. She walked up to it. All the room numbers and levels were marked out: the pool area, the buffet restaurant, the lobby, and the engine room. That was where they needed to go. They had to stop the engine from starting so the cruise ship wouldn't leave port. She pressed her finger on the spot marked "Engine Room."

"Down there," Ebony said.

They walked through the buffet restaurant. Rows of dishes were sitting behind glass cabinets, ready for when the hordes of hungry passengers returned. There was every kind of food imaginable: tacos in the Mexican stand, curries and rice in the Indian section, fish and chips, and pizza. There was even a whole section just for fruit salads and desserts.

"Can you believe all this food?" Ebony asked Jay.

There was no answer. Ebony stopped. Jay was nowhere to be seen. Then she caught sight of him. He had his nose pressed up against the burger counter.

"Jay!" she called, pulling him out of his food daydream.

"Sorry," he said, turning around and running after her.

They kept walking through the ship, going down to the lower levels. Soon they came to a door marked "Engine Room."

Ebony pulled the big handle down, ignoring the sign underneath that said "Staff Only."

It was dark inside the room, after the brightly lit ship, with only a dim yellow light shining. Ebony and Jay's shoes banged noisily on the mesh that covered the floor, as they climbed down to where the engine was. She was amazed at its size, it was bigger than a truck. Thick black oily drops fell like dark teardrops from the engine and through the mesh covering below.

Ebony pulled her cell phone from her pocket. She switched on the torch app and shone it through the mesh. Underneath she could see the whole system. There was a pump and a big tank under there. A tube came out of the tank that was being fed into a drum.

"So that's how they get the waste oil into the drums," Jay said.

It had the same writing on it as the others: "Waste." Ebony took a photo of it. *It must be the last drum that is about to be emptied into the sea,* she thought. Then they heard the engine room door opening.

"Someone's coming!" Jay exclaimed. "Quick, we have to hide."

They snuck behind the machinery. Ebony switched off the torch app, held her breath and pressed "Voice record" on her phone.

The two men from before entered. Ebony stifled a gasp. She realized now that they must be crewmen on the ship. They were heading over to the drum. The men were talking.

"Boy, am I glad this is the last of the drums," the first man said. He pulled out the tube and sealed the drum.

"Yeah, I've got a stiff back from all the lifting," the second man added.

"Shame we couldn't empty all the drums

straight into the sea. That was much easier than emptying them up in the dunes."

"Yeah. And never found that missing drum, either."

"Ah, no problem. Nobody will go up into those back dunes. There's nothing there except a few stupid pelicans."

The men laughed.

"Let's tell the boss it's all done. I'll empty this one overboard once we sail out."

The men left the engine room. Ebony felt the heat rising in her face. She was so angry. How could they deliberately pollute the water and her beach? Why would they do such a thing? She thought of Poseidon and how he had nearly died because of the oil he got covered in. She stopped the recording and slipped her phone back in her pocket.

"How can we stop them emptying that drum into the sea?" Ebony said.

Jay looked around. "I've got an idea!"

"That's the generator. It's just like the one we take camping, only bigger," Jay said, pointing to a big metal piece of equipment. "If we turn it off, the ship will lose power."

"Hey! What are you two doing in here?"

Ebony and Jay spun around. A security guard was standing over them.

"Nothing! W-we, um, got l-lost," Jay stammered.

"Yeah, we couldn't find our cabin. Silly us," Ebony said.

The guard looked them up and down suspiciously. "It's dangerous for you kids to be down here. Where are your ID tags?"

"We, er, left them in our cabin," Jay said.

"Then how were you going to get back into your cabin without your swipe card?" the guard said, eyebrows raised.

Ebony hadn't thought of that when they started making up their story. She didn't know you needed an ID card to get into a cruise cabin.

"We were going to meet our parents there," she said quickly.

The guard frowned and unclipped a radio from his belt. "I'm going to have to check this with the front desk. What are your names?"

Ebony and Jay looked at each other and nodded.

"We're the Eco Rangers!" Jay cried.

Then they made a run for it.

"Hey! Stop!" the guard yelled, chasing after them.

But Ebony and Jay quickly found their way out of the engine room, and began weaving their way back through the passageways of the ship. They could hear the guard calling for extra security on his radio as he puffed along behind them. They were faster than the guard though, and there was soon some distance between them. They turned a corner, then ran up a stairway. The doors of an elevator opposite opened. Out came the two crewmen who had been in the engine room.

The guard yelled out with his last bit of breath as he climbed the stairs: "Stop them!"

The crewmen ran toward Ebony and Jay and grabbed hold of them.

"Let go of me!" Ebony yelled, as one of the men gripped her arm tightly. The other one held Jay by the back of his T-shirt. The guard made it to the landing at the top of the stairs. He clipped his radio back on his belt.

"Thanks," he said to the crewmen, red-faced and puffing.

"We'll take them from here," one of them said. "You kids again… Come on! You two stowaways have a lot of explaining to do."

Ebony looked at Jay. They were really in trouble now.

The two Eco Rangers were led down several passageways until they came to an office door. It had a shiny gold plaque on it with the word "MANAGER" in capital letters. This was not good. One of the crewmen knocked on the door.

A voice from the other side said, "Enter."

The door swung open and the man with the slicked-back hair and business suit stood there scowling at them. It was the cruise ship manager. Ebony tried to pull away from the crewman, but he was too strong for her and he pushed her roughly into the room. The other man followed, letting go of Jay as he closed and locked the door behind them.

"The guard found these two stowing away. They were sneaking around in the engine room when he found 'em," the crewman said.

"Don't they look familiar to you?" the other crewman said.

"You're the kids that were sneaking around my truck!" the manager cried.

He moved so close to Ebony as he spat out his words that she could smell his tuna breath. Yuck!

"Yeah, and now we know it's true you're dumping the oil. Deliberately," Jay said. "You can't get away with it. We even have proof. We took—"

Ebony glared at Jay. All they had as evidence was the voice recording and photos she had taken. She didn't want these men knowing she had proof.

"You took what?" the manager said slyly.

"Um, ah, we took a pelican that was

covered in oil to the wildlife hospital," Ebony said hastily.

"Really? And didn't you hear that it was an oil leak and it's all fixed now?"

"Yes, but we heard these men saying they were dumping the oil," Jay said, pointing to the two men blocking the doorway.

Without thinking, Ebony touched the pocket where her phone was. The manager noticed and a smile formed on his thin lips.

"And what is it you have in your pocket, young lady?" he said.

"Nothing," Ebony replied.

"Give it to me," he yelled.

Ebony removed the phone from her pocket. The manager snatched it from her.

"You won't be needing this."

He shoved her phone in his jacket pocket. Ebony let out a little cry.

"You know what I think? I think you two have been put up to this. I think you people don't like the tourists coming to your precious little town and you and your friends are a bunch of troublemakers. And you know what happens to troublemakers around here?"

"What?" Ebony asked.

"We keep them quiet!"

Ebony looked at Jay, wide-eyed.

"Yes, I can see the headline now," the cruise ship manager said, rubbing his hands together. "Two stowaways found safe and well by ship manager after spending four days out at sea."

"You can't do that!" Ebony screamed.

"Yeah, that's ... that's kidnapping," Jay agreed.

"Oh, yes, I can," the man sneered. "And I know exactly what I'll say to the news reporters. Want to hear it?"

Ebony and Jay both shook their heads. He cleared his throat as if he was about to make a speech and said dramatically, "The two stowaways were found living off scraps from the buffet. Luckily a crewman found them when they were scrounging for food. We are so glad we could return them safely to their worried families." He laughed. "Oh, yes, I'll be the hero of this story and no one will ever believe two lying stowaways that we dumped oil waste."

"Why would you do that?" Ebony cried. "You're harming the animals and polluting the sea."

"So? A little bit of oil waste in the sea is better than paying the huge amount of money they want to charge me at the waste disposal center. It's saving *me* money, lots of glorious money, dumping the oil waste myself."

"You'll never get away with it," Ebony cried, not so sure.

"Yes, I will," the man sneered in return. "You don't have your phone either, so you won't be able to contact anyone!"

The Eco Rangers gulped. Ebony's legs

started to shake, and Jay looked as white as Poseidon's feathers. The manager turned to the crewmen.

"Get rid of these kids. Cabin 525 is empty. You can put them in there."

The crewmen took Ebony and Jay down to the empty cabin and shoved them inside roughly.

"I don't suppose we could have some of those chocolate chip cookies while we're waiting to be rescued?" Jay asked.

The men just laughed and closed the door on them. Ebony tried to open it but the cabin had been locked from the outside. They were trapped.

Ebony looked around. The cabin had four bunk beds and a set of drawers in the middle. There was a door to a small bathroom in the corner, two wardrobes, and a dresser. There was no phone, though.

"What now?" Jay asked.

Ebony stared out of the small porthole at the empty sea and shrugged. She had no idea how they were going to get out of this one.

"I need the toilet," Jay said, opening the door to the small bathroom.

Ebony sighed and continued looking out to sea. Then she glanced at the small clock hanging between the beds. The ship was about to sail. They had to get out of there, fast. Suddenly she thought she saw something. She squinted her eyes against the sun. Yes, there was something in the sky. A white dot. It was getting larger. It was a huge bird. She knew that bird. It was Poseidon! She started banging on the window and waving her arms at him. He flew closer and came in to land on the porthole ledge. He tapped the glass with his big bill. She heard the toilet flush and Jay came out, wiping his hands on his shorts.

"Look who's here," she said.

"Poseidon!" Jay exclaimed. "He must have finished his egg-sitting duties."

The pelican stayed a few more minutes and then flew back out to sea. Ebony wished he could have helped them escape.

Ebony couldn't help herself. She started to cry. They were never going to get out of there. Jay put his hand on her shaking shoulder.

"It'll be all right," he said. "In a few days, we'll be back home and everything will work out. You'll see."

Ebony wiped her eyes with the back of her hand.

"Our parents will be so worried about us."

An announcement rang out through the ship's system: "We will be getting under way shortly. Please come up on deck to enjoy our sail-away party. The weather is lovely and it's looking like a beautiful afternoon, so bring your cameras and don't forget to put on your dancing shoes. See you there."

"If only we could get up on deck." Ebony sighed.

She dropped back on the crisp white sheets, her head resting on the soft pillow. She crossed her arms over her chest and closed her eyes.

Ebony must have drifted off to sleep on the comfortable bed for a few minutes because the next thing she knew she was awoken by a tapping sound at the porthole. Half-asleep, she pulled herself up and glanced over. It was Poseidon again. He hadn't left them after all! He was tapping his bill on the round window. Then he flew away again. Ebony pressed her face against the glass. She could see the jetty far below. A group of people were running up and down the port. They had their hands cupped over their mouths like they were calling out. Ebony realized what Poseidon had been doing. He had been trying to tell their parents where they were!

"We're going to be rescued!" she said to Jay. "Thanks to one smart pelican."

Excited, Ebony and Jay banged on the window. But the figures were too far away. They couldn't see them, and even if they could, they'd never make it before the ship sailed. She and Jay stopped waving. They weren't going to be rescued after all, no one had seen them up here. They'd sail off and no one would find them till the next port, days later.

"It's hopeless," Ebony said, slumping back on her bed.

"There has to be another way out of here," Jay said.

He walked around the room, searched the bathroom and opened the closet. He went to open a second door next to the dresser.

"I wonder what this wardrobe's for?" Jay turned the handle. "It's locked." He sighed.

Ebony jumped up. "That's not a wardrobe, that's a door. We're in a connecting cabin."

"Then there must be a way of opening it," Jay said.

Ebony looked at the door. There was a metal slot on one side.

"We need the key card to unlock it," she said.

They searched the cabin, opening cupboard doors and drawers, but they couldn't see a key card. Finally, Jay found the welcome folder in the safe that was kept open, ready for the next guests. There was a card tucked neatly inside it. He picked it up. "This could be it."

Ebony grabbed it from him and placed the card in the slot on the door. It fitted! The door lock clicked. Ebony pushed the door open, pressed her fingers to her lips and waved for Jay to follow. They snuck into the adjoining room. It was empty.

The Eco Rangers tiptoed to the front of the cabin. Ebony pulled down the door handle, and it unlocked. They were free.

The friends looked left and right down the passageway, and started running, following the signs to the gangway exit. They raced past cabins, sprinted down stairways, and along hallways, to the main atrium. They reached the spiral staircase leading to the lobby. There were people everywhere, listening to a pianist playing, sipping drinks and chatting among themselves. Ebony looked at a gigantic white and gold clock hanging on the wall. They had only minutes before the ship would depart. They had to get to the gangway.

"This way!" she yelled to Jay.

The Eco Rangers headed straight through the middle of the busy lobby, toward the buffet restaurant. Ebony noticed a steward talking into his radio, but she thought nothing of it. They turned the corner toward the restaurant. They weaved between people carrying plates piled high with food, and guests eating at the tables. They were nearly through! Then they just had to go past the outdoor area and down the stairs to the gangway. They were going to make it!

"Oh, no!" Jay said, grabbing Ebony's arm. "They're here!"

Ebony turned. It was the manager and the two crewmen.

"Get them!" the manager yelled.

The two crewmen stormed toward the Eco Rangers. Ebony and Jay ran. The men broke into a run too, knocking into guests. Ebony looked over her shoulder to see one of the men send a woman's plate of spaghetti flying in the air. It landed on the floor, and the man slipped straight on the gooey pasta, falling with a thud. The other man was still running after them, though. Ebony and Jay ducked around a waiter carrying a cake, but the man wasn't as quick as them. He rammed into the waiter. The waiter spun around and the cake went flying, straight into the man's face. He yelled and wiped cake from his eyes.

Ebony and Jay raced out of the restaurant and bolted across the pool area. They dodged deck chairs with people sunbathing, and small, round tables with people sitting around them. But the two men, splattered with food, were gaining on them again. The manager wasn't far behind. They were never going to make it!

Then Ebony saw a staff member hosing down the pool edge where a toddler had dropped his ice cream. She quickly snatched the hose from him and sprayed water at the men. They slipped and slid on the slippery floor, waving their arms in the air. The two men fell into each other, wobbled on the edge of the pool, and fell in.

"Arrgh! Somebody get those kids!" the manager screamed.

The guests looked at the man in the suit strangely and went back to reading, swimming and drinking colorful drinks with straws and pieces of pineapple on top. The Eco Rangers made it to the other end of the pool area and pushed open the glass doors. They went straight to the stairs and ran down to the gangway. The manager chased behind. There were two security officers standing at the exit, in front of the scanning machines.

"We need to get off!" Ebony puffed.

"I'm sorry but the ship is about to leave," one officer said. "We're closing the gangway."

"It's an emergency!" Jay screamed.

The two officers looked at each other.

One shrugged.

"Don't … let … them … through!" The now red-faced manager had caught up with them and was gasping for breath. "Close the gangway."

Oh no! Ebony's eyes stung with tears. They had been so close to making it off.

The sopping wet and angry crewmen had caught up too, and now roughly grabbed hold of Ebony and Jay.

"Take them back to the cabin," the manager commanded.

Ebony sighed helplessly as one of the security officers gave the signal to close the gangway. She looked down the ramp connecting the ship to the shore as they were dragged away. Then she saw a blur of wings heading in their direction.

Poseidon swooped toward the ship, glided up the gangway and flew over their heads. He landed between the gobsmacked security guards. He spread his wings wide and whacked the security guards in the face.

"What's going on." the manager screeched.

"Poseidon, you found us!" Ebony cried.

The pelican strutted in a circle, making a squeaky calling sound.

Ebony's mom and Jay's parents came running up the gangway, following the sound of the squawking pelican. Poseidon had led them to the Eco Rangers!

"Get that bird out of here," the manager yelled. "Then close the gangway."

"No!" Ebony yelled.

Two police officers came running up behind the parents.

"Keep the gangway open," said the police.

The manager took one look at the angry crowd storming toward him and ran in the opposite direction. The police chased after him, catching up with the panting manager before he reached the end of the passageway. They put the red-faced man in handcuffs.

The police asked what had happened as they dragged the manager back to the ship's entrance. Ebony and Jay quickly told them.

"How do you explain holding two children on board against their will?" the female police officer said to the cruise ship manager.

"They're stowaways. I didn't even know they were on board," the manager insisted.

Ebony slowly realized it would be his word against theirs. Which reminded her—the only evidence she had was on her cell phone.

"Check his jacket pocket," Ebony said to the police officer. "My phone's in there. It has a hot-pink cover. He took it from me. It has all the evidence you need about them dumping the oil waste."

The manager's face turned pale as the police told him to empty his pockets. Sure enough, he pulled out Ebony's pink phone. The male police officer took it from him.

"That's my personal property," the manager insisted.

"Hot-pink cover? It's just like she said. So, what do we have here?" the officer said, as he started listening to the recording and looking at the pictures on Ebony's phone. His face grew darker and darker as he listened and scrolled through the images.

"It's off to the police station for you," the police officer said, leading the scowling manager out. The security guards stared at each other in disbelief.

Meanwhile, Ebony and Jay's parents had bundled their kids up in a huge hug. Then they all made their way off the ship, talking and asking questions. Ebony had never been happier to feel her feet on dry land.

Poseidon spread his wings wide beside them and strutted around them proudly.

"Poseidon!" Ebony cried to her feathered friend. She and Jay went up to him and stroked his feathers. He nuzzled into the Eco Rangers.

"You really saved us!" Jay said.

"Yes, thank you, Poseidon!" Ebony exclaimed.

Before Ebony knew it, sunlight was streaming through her bedroom window and her mom was gently shaking her awake.

"It's breakfast time, Eco Ranger," her mom whispered.

Ebony pulled her quilt over her head and rolled over. She still felt tired after all that had happened. As soon as they'd got home from being rescued off the cruise ship she'd gone straight to sleep. Her mom shook her again.

"Come on! There's someone waiting for you downstairs."

Ebony groaned again and pulled herself out of bed.

She smiled through bleary eyes when she saw Jay sitting at the kitchen table. He was piling toast onto his plate and smearing it with a generous serving of peanut butter.

"Sorry, couldn't wait, I'm starving," he said, biting the corner off his dripping toast.

"What are you doing here?" Ebony laughed.

"I woke up early and couldn't think of anything better to do." He shrugged.

Ebony took a piece of toast and put it on her plate, too. It all seemed like a dream, and she wondered how they'd been found in the end.

"How did you know we were on the ship?" Ebony asked her mom.

"The persistence of one special bird," she replied. Ebony frowned and her mom explained. "Poseidon came back home without you or Jay. He kept squawking and flapping about. I asked him where you were but of course he couldn't answer, so I followed him all the way to the beach and down to the jetty. When I reached the cruise ship terminal, I found your sweater lying on the ground but there was no sign of you. That's when I knew something was wrong. I tried to call you but you didn't answer your phone. I called Jay's parents, who called the police. Then Poseidon kept flying back and forth to the porthole on the ship, and we knew you must be on board. The rest you know."

Just as she reached for the peanut butter there was a tapping sound on the back door.

"Who could that be now?" her mom said.

"I'll check," Ebony said.

She pushed back her chair and went to the door. She was surprised to see Doctor Bat and Doctor Tan standing there.

Ebony's mom gestured for them to come in. They sat down, and joined them for toast—and coffee for the adults. The vets explained how the cruise ship manager had been trying to cut costs by emptying the oil waste straight into the sea instead of paying to dispose of it properly. Once the oil had started washing up on shore they had lied and said they had an oil leak. Then they had to get rid of it another way, and that was when they had started dumping it behind the dunes.

"The photos and voice recording you took gave the police all the information they needed," Doctor Bat said.

"Not only are the manager and his two crewmen in trouble with the police, but the cruise ship company has fined them as well," Doctor Tan said.

"And they'll have to pay to clean up the dunes," Doctor Bat added.

"So, the cruise ship company wasn't to blame?" Ebony asked.

"No, they had no idea. The manager was keeping the money he saved on waste removal for himself," Doctor Bat said. "He was going to split the money with the two engine room crew, who were helping."

"That's who he must have been talking to on the phone the other day!" Jay said. "He was telling them to fill the drums so they could dump the oil behind the dunes."

"Oh, that reminds me. I have something for you." Doctor Bat reached into her large bag. She pulled out two pieces of thick card and handed one to each of the Eco Rangers. Ebony was the first to read the ticket and she squealed excitedly.

"Ouch! You're hurting my ears," Jay complained. Then he looked at his ticket. "Wow! An annual pass to Super World theme park. You're the best. Thank you!"

"It's just a small thanks from the center, and hopefully it'll be nice to have some fun after all that hard work looking after your feisty pelican friend." Doctor Bat grinned.

"What about Poseidon?" Ebony said. "Is he okay?"

"He was a little tired after leaving his enclosure a bit too soon. But he's doing well and is back on the beach," Doctor Tan said. "Would you like to see him?"

Ebony and Jay looked at each other and both said together, "We'd love to!"

The two friends walked up the beach toward the dunes. Then Ebony heard a kind of swooshing sound. A white head appeared from behind the dunes.

"Poseidon!" she yelled.

Ebony raced along the beach to meet her friend. The pelican moved from foot to foot and pushed his bill against Ebony until she stumbled back. Poseidon started tugging on the sleeve of her sweater.

"I think he wants us to follow him," Jay exclaimed.

Ebony followed Poseidon up the beach to the dunes.

Jay puffed along behind. "Wait for me!"

When Ebony got to the top, she found out the reason Poseidon had wanted them to come up to the dunes. As she got closer, she noticed there was something moving. She looked more closely. Wait! There was a small shape next to the pelican mom. The baby! It was just like its parents, only smaller and fluffier, with soft downy feathers.

Jay came up next to Ebony and crouched down on the sand.

"He's a dad!" Jay exclaimed.

"Aw, isn't it the cutest?" Ebony said.

Poseidon nudged them as if to say he

agreed. They both stroked him gently, showing how much they cared. Being an Eco Ranger was the best job ever!